DEAR

X

Dear X

Jumanah Al Saihati
translated by
Ola Ali Hassan

DEAR X
Jumanah Al Saihati

First published in Arabic by Nadhd Publishing in 2021
Published by Nomad Publishing in 2024
Email: info@nomad-publishing.com
www.nomad-publishing.com

ISBN 978-1-914325-31-1

© Jumanah Al Saihati 2024

Cover design: Richard Budd

 The Publishers would like to thank the Harf Literary Agency

Disclaimer: the content and any opinions included in such content reflect the views and opinions of the author and do not reflect the opinions and beliefs of the publisher, the translator, Tarjim program, or any of their affiliates. The author is solely responsible for any statements made in such content and any translation is made based on the perception of the author from the original language or source of information prior to any translation or adaptation made.
CIP Data: A catalogue for this book is available from the British Library

For those who were drained by COVID-19 and whose words were suppressed.
I am one of them.
Believe me, it was not easy.

2020

Her room had a single, lonely window, like a yellow flower growing on top of a cactus otherwise covered with spines and prickles. The window looked over a world overwhelmed by tremendous stress and anxiety, and while she had loads of unanswered questions, she also feared finding answers to those questions. She put her hand on her stomach and felt the sensation of fear consistently striking her guts, like a foetus kicking its mother. She sat on the edge of the bed, experiencing the strange feeling of someone sitting on the edge of the world. She was scared to move lest she fall, but the whole world had already begun to fall to the bottom of a pandemic that was vigorously devouring bodies and lives imprisoned by fear.

"COVID-19." She pronounced the term as though it were the codename of a military mission that could happen only in a Hollywood movie. That codename occupied news bulletins, newspapers, and online journals, and dominated the conversations of families and neighbours. The codename was disseminated everywhere and by every imaginable means. The entire world was on alert, wrapped in darkness in anticipation of calamity falling on the heads of its inhabitants, who lived in fear of death. She articulated the dread term again, this time slowly, like a first-grade student struggling to get the pronunciation just right, and she wondered how the alphabet could produce such a hideous, scary term, a term that made people fear each other!

She stood up and eyed the window suspiciously. Then she covered it over with wooden boards, nailing each one into place for fear that a ray of light might slip through. She tried to cut every connection between herself and the city outside the walls of her home. She had started writing letters to a man far away, distanced from her by the pandemic. She wrote letters on paper in a time when postmen no longer existed and had been replaced by inanimate digital applications that ignored emotions, worries, and fears.

She was living a cloistered life, isolated and separated from everything and everyone, part of her wishing she could go back in time. She was waiting for the pandemic to end because although she had shuttered the window, the spectre of calamity still dominated her soul and dominated the wall, just as it dominated information spaces. She could feel the fear spreading and splintering throughout her body, to her vocal cords, the layers of her skin, and the strands of her hair. She paced back and forth across the room, unaware that the floor was turning into water and that every step brought her closer to drowning. Everything became slimy and faded in colour, everything except her letters, which she kept writing even as she sank ever deeper.

MARCH

G ood morning,

I want to write you a letter this morning.

I woke up early, and the feeling of longing is irritating me, hurting me. Even though I hate this feeling, it creates a vivid picture of you, and I wish I could touch you through that painful picture. I know you miss me, even if you prefer to keep such feelings to yourself, and even if I don't understand why you don't share your feelings, since life is short, as you can see. It can put barriers between us, accursed barriers which we cannot pass without a miracle. These barriers came in the form of a pandemic that has locked the whole world up in isolated shells. I must confess, however, that this is my only consolation for not being able to see you.

I know no other way to tell you that I miss you because that nasty digital chat fails to deliver feelings. It can't communicate the feeling of desolation that hacks up my throat, the itchiness in my hands because they crave touching you, or the widening of my eyes because they are eager to see you. We were not created for this! I barely feel the hankering inspired by even the most timeless of Arabic poetry. It tastes sour in my mouth.

Tell me about you, and I will tell you about the things that scared me and deprived me of the tranquillity of your presence. I will look for a way to explain all of that while reserving the question of "how?" I mean, how can I explain the feelings of a thirty-year-old woman looking for something or someone to share her burdens with her without giving up or falling?

That moment eventually arrived when the first case was announced in our city, like a dream slapping everyone out of their sleep. This moment woke me up, triggering a delusional survival instinct inside me. For what survival I am begging for when I shelter behind a closed window, blinded to the world and away from you, and when the only connection between us is what is written on the internet?

Oh, my Goodness! I am sinking in a sea of human beings, and I wish I could give you my hand, but I fear you won't stretch yours out to grasp mine. Then, after long conversations with myself and after clinging to the hope that you have the same feelings towards me, I prefer to keep my letter without sending it.

Anyway, I don't think you'd waste your time reading a

DEAR X

paper letter among the many streams of digital chats and character-limited texts, all of which have taught us to be brief. Even when conveying love.

Therefore, I will stop now. I will end my letter and keep the rest in my heart. I might choke on it or cry over it for a long time, but that is totally fine. I also want to tell you that I am with you, though, and amidst all that chaos that has somehow suddenly struck the whole world, I will stay by your side. I fear, however, that you won't give me a hand.

I love you so much, even in your silence and in mine ...

Sara

Good morning again,

I must tell you that writing yesterday's letter has revived my soul and cheered me up. It awoke something inside me. I must admit I missed writing on paper. Sadly, you won't be able to read it, but that's okay. I can move on when I sink into my thoughts and remember that you don't like long reads.

What is the point of falling in love with a writer then? Nonetheless, writing to you made me breathe freely despite the stifled air we are breathing these days. Writing is also a lot easier than using my voice, which often betrays me in your presence, falling down like autumn leaves and making it hard to deliver what I try to say.

I think I must choose a name for you so that beginning my letters will be easier. A name you won't recognize, like an undefined value in a mathematical equation. What do you think of "X"? It's the same obscure value we wasted our lives trying in vain to define, just like you.

I got used to staying on the waiting list while you carried on with your life. Could it be possible that you are unaware that I am waiting for you? Or have you willingly chosen to ignore it? Thinking of this drowns me in the deepest seas of sadness. You are being unfair to me, and for some reason, I think you know. Oppressive people are always aware that they are being unfair but pretend the opposite.

Wanted to say good morning.

That's all.

Sara

Dear X,

The world went crazy and days melted together. The morning was no longer meaningful; even "good morning" withered away, and the same went for "good evening."

Can you believe that?

I haven't asked myself this before, but what if life in the city stopped and grief suddenly befell it?

That grief came down repeatedly, every afternoon at four, when the curfew was imposed. The city would feel stressed and troubled by fever. It would wish its streets could get dusted away to diminish the pandemic that had confined its people and kept me from you. Now the city is sad, wrapped in a wind that whistles through empty streets, looking for a woman's dress to flutter or a child's kite to blow.

Everything is coloured with the dusky stress, even the trees that adorn the streets, and the traffic lights that still glow despite the absence of vehicles.

Another misery emerges from the roads at six in the morning. You feel the hurried steps of those who fear touching or being touched. You listen in vain for the usual noise of buses or traffic jams. The lockdown hours have been eased a bit, but they soon return with even heavier dismay than before.

I don't think I've ever thought about the sadness of my city or the possibility that its life may freeze, even temporarily, because I was busy with my grief and my longing for you, which stays trapped inside my letters. However, this made me a selfish human being.

I can assure you that the city cries when it is ignored, deserted, and denied attention. It cries when it sees the children kept home from their schools, and the companies and other organizations limiting the numbers of employees who can come to work.

My city's despair at midnight is yet another story. People's eyes don't sleep, and the city cannot sleep either. Sleep also brings its own stories and difficulties, which everyone is afraid to confess. We've never got used to the quietness of the streets, creeping into our souls like silent chaos and leaving us sleepless.

You will say that I am describing a whole nation. Yes ... I can even certify that this is the whole world's situation, in all these cities where that disease has crouched like an

DEAR X

unwanted guest, refusing to leave until it has inflicted maximum losses. We are all bearing our losses, living in mourning and fear.

The one whose life is lived in fear,

Sara

Dear X,

It is still well before dawn now, thirty minutes past 1 a.m. according to my watch, and this is a convenient time to tell you that I have been searching for you, but my efforts have been useless. How is it possible for your mobile phone to embrace the whole world but exclude me? I have been asking myself this question again and again, but I'm afraid to ask you lest your brutal honesty break me.

I am scared, X; I am looking forward to the security of your chest to shelter me, without which I am paralyzed by my fear. The whole world is dark, and the whole darkness of the world has settled inside me, as if I were an endless night and you were the moon hiding behind the shadow of the sun, not because of an eclipse, but because it was escaping.

Tell me about dawn; how does it pass when I am not around?

The eternal searcher for you,

Sara

Dear X,

Death is our ultimate destiny. It does not separate us, as the common notion suggests, but rather, it takes us to different dimensions. Perhaps it reactivates the actions of guilt, nostalgia, and prayer. It is life that causes separation and imposes parting. It whips our backs with the nonsense that puts us at crossroads. It tells us the lie that no one stands for another, and we naively believe it, allowing this to be imposed as a rule to which all human relationships shall adhere.

Our existence becomes a burden, and we no longer give a helping hand to others. We turn our backs in the blink of an eye, as letting go is easier than holding on, even if holding on is what we deeply desire. We invoke ego and pride, and we let go! Life lets go of us in return. Who could have believed that we would be locked down in a mandatory quarantine for health reasons? Death has always been closer and easier to believe.

Death is the only available option, while life shuts its doors in our faces, one after the other; it waves us goodbye every day, even if we have never noticed. Only the dead are aware of this. Death is the first and last experience, resolving what we have been concerned and anxious about, even our places in the hearts of others: when we die, we become dear.

Sara

APRIL

DEAR X

G ood evening, dear X,

I have not written to you for a couple of mornings, but your voice seeped into my ears yesterday and flowed through my veins and into my organs like still water. I felt like a pure colour had spread through my blood until my face glowed. I am coloured with the tint of happiness, the happiness that had been about to fade until your voice brought it back in one minute and twenty-four seconds. It seems that I will succumb, after all, to the attempts of modern technology to minimize sounds and words, as I had not imagined the extent of the rejoice I would feel at hearing your voice!

The rejoicer at the colour of your voice,

Sara

DEAR X

D ear X,

The rain visited us today. It fell on the empty streets while the terrified people of the pandemic watched it from behind their windows. As for me, since I boarded up my window, I have been paying much attention to the noises of the outside world. I wait for the sound of the rain, which draws a smile on my face and reminds me of your voice.

Do you know the "Rain Song" poem? When the great poet Al-Sayyab asks his greatest question? "Do you know how lost a lonely person feels in the rain?"

Now I wish I were a poet so I could tell him that I do.

Do you remember the rhythm of the rain falling on our smiles for the first time while we were together? I told you that I was going to untie my hair and run around you under the rain. You laughed and warned me about slipping, and when I followed your warning, afraid that I would fall, you whispered, "Do you fear while you are with me?" I have never been afraid as long as you were by my side, but afraid is all that I feel now!

Do not worry. Send me a message and tell me about the rain where you are. Have you known how lost a lonely person feels in the rain?

The one who heard the rain but has not felt its consolation,

Sara

G ood morning, X,

The rain poured and poured, stroking the heads of the houses for days before it stopped. Yesterday I was pacing my room, back and forth, until I realized that I had forgot it had a door. When the realization occurred to me, I was struck by a yearning to grip the doorknob. The knob was warm and of a faded golden colour that has lost its shine. I felt as though it had missed the texture of my hand. I opened it slowly, trying to cherish a moment that used to be very basic and very typical. But every basic thing and every routine action has been missed. I mean, who could ever have imagined that these non-negotiable things would become scarce, dwindle, and disappear?

I climbed up to the roof of the building where I live, where piles of wet sand accumulated in its corners. I raised my head to the rainbow of colours that declared the end of the downpour. I smiled, and for a moment I forgot all the sorrows that I wrote to you in my previous letter. I walked slowly, trying to leave my footprints on the piles of sand. I could see a black beetle walking through the grains of sand next to the wall. It had six legs, which were shiny, as if they had never touched sand or dirt. I squatted down to watch it more closely and was reminded of "The Metamorphosis," the famous Franz Kafka story in which the main character becomes an insect. I imagined for a moment how I would feel if my arms and legs transformed into insect limbs, and the idea scared me so much that I instinctively wiped off my hands, even though they were perfectly clean.

Tell me, have you read "The Metamorphosis"? I know you tend not to like absurd story lines, and that you have stopped reading quite some time ago, even though you used to try relentlessly to read me, so that your line, "how wonderful to be loved by a writer," would be more meaningful.

Later on, I searched for the beetle, but it was nowhere to be found. I believe that staying under the control of solitude will throw me into the world of absurdity! Can the beetle feel terror when it sees someone huge heading towards it, like I did when I imagined this tiny thing crawling on my hand? Or perhaps it imagines itself turning into a human being who practices all sorts of absence and emotional injustice, so it becomes proud of its species.

Anyway, you ought to read the novel.

Sara

It is Dawn Now.

X, this time I will not say "dear". But I swear by the one who instilled you in the place of my soul that you are the dearest of all where my heart belongs. I am going to skip this word for now though, at least in this letter. I do not think you notice my absence from you, and I do not ask you for that either, since I already know the answer, just as you do. I rather believe that you are forcibly blocking the way before me.

I talk to myself every night. I will stop searching for you, seeing you in the books I read, and waiting for your name to pop up on my mobile screen. I will do my best to skip your memory, but birds of a feather flock together, and I – who once thought of myself as a bird spreading its wings up in your sky – have crashed terribly. I have flocked with someone who is not alike, and the winds that once lifted me up have stopped blowing and hastened my fall, a fall that I would not wish on my worst enemy.

D^{ear} X,

It's a neutral time of the day, neither night nor morning, the exact time when we were chatting like lovebirds, warbling in the early stages of love. You were talking to me passionately, while I was answering shyly. You called to me with poetic odes, and I dodged the answers with a trick that both of us knew you would not believe. I tried to hide behind my words, and even though it was obvious that I sought only to extract more warm ones from you, you nonetheless obliged me, like a father who has never denied a request from his daughter. How mind-blowing that fortune can gift you the treasure of love and then suddenly pull it back, as though it had never been given to you!

I am searching for a suitable way to approach you, but I keep returning empty-handed. I tell myself that you will be the one in charge of the conversation this time, but such a thing has never happened. I might send you a song so it could be the centre of our discussion, but I've already tried that before, and that discussion is also yet to take place. Were I to count the things that have not happened, I reckon I would not stop.

Sara

Good morning,

What if I quit writing?

I don't mean just my letters to you, but writing in general. Would the number of local literati decrease, or am I somewhat overvaluing myself?

I admit that writing is exhausting and not as easy as I had originally thought. I used to think it was no more than a stress reliever, but after I finished my first book, I found my wounds splintering, their pain spreading all over my guts. I bore loads of sorrows on my shoulders, so much that it felt like these sorrows had only been created so writers around the world could share in them. You find that each and every writer has his or her own burden of sorrows whose weight bends their backs, and I cannot drop mine now. The way back has vanished, and the way forward is rough and muddy. Stopping makes me feel like an ancient building that has long withstood the forces of time but is now so eroded that it begins to crumble.

If I did stop writing, would you ask me one day why I had stopped? Would you put my hand to it again? Or would it not bother you at all?

The latter choice seems the most probable in my opinion, but I will deceive myself and flatter myself a little bit. I will say that you would take my hand and ask me insistently about my next piece of literary work, even if you have never read any previous pieces of mine before.

The writer who fears to quit,
but intends to ...

Sara

MAY

D ear X,

I wanted to get out today, to face the outside world that has been devastated more by the fear of the pandemic than the pandemic itself. In fact, this was not out of audacity; rather, I needed some supplies. Ramadan has come, as you know, and I needed some fresh air as well.

I put my mask on my face and felt like a wanted criminal who purposely hides from people's eyes. I wore gloves so nothing could touch my skin, and I smelled like alcohol. I wore my watch too, although I have always thought of it as a restraint on my wrist and a reminder that I am running out of time. This time was different, though, as I needed to be aware of the leakage of time and make sure I would return before five o'clock.

The street looked so vast, and I couldn't remember ever seeing it this way. I'm not sure if it has always been that wide, or if the paucity of people gave it the chance to stretch itself out. Sunlight scratched at my eyes. I had forgotten how much feeling I formerly attached to it, and it seems that it forgot me as well, or maybe it was punishing me for boarding up my window and refusing to receive its shining rays. The city was not as empty as I had thought, although the people who were out literally made themselves scarce by fearfully running away from one another. Apprehension and anxiety were palpable in their eyes, and the smell of alcohol smell emanated from them, too.

I walked quickly, trying not to look at anyone. I walked near walls, trying to avoid touching anything, even the stuff I meant to buy. My hands were sweating whenever I tried to touch anything, so I took my gloves off. As soon as I returned home, I stuffed my outer clothes into a black plastic bag and hurried into the shower.

That was an adventure that I fear repeating.

Have you tried going out as well? Did you fear people as I did, or do I tend to exaggerate?

Sara the Adventurous

Dear X,

How are you today? Haven't you missed me yet?

I swear to God that each day, I miss you more than ever before. It is midnight, and I feel pains exhausting my body. If we were like before, I would tell you about my exhaustion, and you would reply with your usual compassion, assuring me that everything would be fine, and that rest was all I needed. You would ask me about the reasons why I refuse to visit a doctor. I would answer that I prefer not to, so before going to bed you would ask me another time how I was feeling and then scold me, saying, "Haven't I told you to see a doctor?" Again, I would tell you, "I'll be better tomorrow."

However, we are not like we used to be, for we have transformed into such an ambiguous form. The long distance between us has defeated us so resoundingly that it makes me wonder: has the pandemic come to reveal our true places, feelings, and identities? I really cannot figure this out, and neither could you work out my last message – in our abandoned chat – which took the form of a joke but which was very real indeed, and I was fully aware of what I had literally said. But you found it funny, and I believe you did that deliberately in order to avoid confrontation.

The words of that joke have departed from the bottom of my heart and snatched some of my organs on their way out. I formed it with a dark colour, but it reached you colourless and even translucent, so allow me to rephrase it here. What if this fatigue was sending me a signal that the pandemic had knocked on the doors of my body? This is the kind of anxiety I have experienced since I put the boards on my window and since you put me on your waiting list.

Damn all these digital chats, for they could never deliver the trembling of my fingers when I write them, nor pass on the shakiness of my vocal cords when I exert myself to swallow my sobs and speak. This is hilarious, a joke in itself!

The resenter of digital chats,

Sara

Good evening, Dear X,

I hope you are still as I have always known you – not on my waiting list, of course, but exactly like you used to be.

I want to tell you that I am terrified that my days may not continue. You have no idea how much and in what form you reside in my heart. Everything that is happening in the world aggravates the feeling of fear inside me. This life is ephemeral, it spares nothing, and I am haunted by the nightmare of being annihilated and forgotten, as though I had never existed. I stopped watching the news, and I'm still locking myself away from everything happening outside, even though it has reached in to where I live. The pandemic is lurking in the shadows, it has entered the homes of my neighbours, and I'll bet I've heard it knocking on my door, which I'm considering boarding up like I did to my window. However, I fear this would widen the distance between you and me, the distance I had never believed in before, but is very real now. So far I am resisting my desire to open your digital chat, which I swore I would not break into, but I am sure that eventually, I will have to expiate the violation of my oath!

I scroll through old photos and try to forget about the pandemic that has started knocking on my door. I wake up in the morning to search for more boards.

Goodnight

Good morning,

Or good afternoon to be more accurate,

Mornings elapse quickly these days, running away with our ages. This is one of the most terrifying facts which the pandemic has brought up.

I mentioned in the letter I wrote to you yesterday that I was thinking of barring the door with wooden boards, but I refrained. I rather intend to leave it ajar now.

The disease might creep in from the neighbours' homes, assuming I have not already brought it in with me from my adventurous trip outside. Isn't facing the dilemma easier than fearfully waiting for it?

I might be invaded by a fever, which I sometimes feel has occupied parts of my body. Perhaps some fatigue and cough, but not a big deal, right?

Anyway, Eid will be at the door in a week I think, and

an official source has indicated that lockdown will be fully imposed for a couple of days. The sorrows of the city will multiply as the celebrations of its inhabitants are shifted online. What an extraordinary Eid!

I am eager to know what kind of Eid is at your door and what kind of fasting you go through.

What about you? Tell me about yourself.

The one who is ready to face the pandemic,

Sara

D^{ear} X,

Good evening, although I am not quite sure of that.

I feel a heaviness in my head, as if I were carrying the entire globe inside. That onerousness has been haunting me for days. If you checked, you'd notice how much our digital chat has become poorly worded, even though it hasn't carried more than passing words for a while.

I don't have the energy to elaborate in writing, or to ask where you are.

What's harder than getting COVID-19 is having to ask for the sympathy of your dearest ones. By the way, I received a message confirming that I tested positive for COVID two or three days ago. I am not certain exactly when. It's not as bad as I feared, maybe somewhat worse. The fever was harsh enough not to have left my body until this very moment, and I am unable to smell. Even those scents which I had always believed to be unforgettable, the ones which used to prompt my memory to retrieve the moments with you, have left my mind.

Can you imagine if scents disappeared from the world? If the perfume preserved inside the folds of our shared memory left it? If the smell of printed paper stopped wafting through the hallways of the library where we used to meet? Or if the sea on whose shores we wetted our bare feet became odourless? Do you think that our ability to heal would be stronger?

Anyway, I will sleep for a bit, hoping these hammers will take a break from constantly tapping on my head.

The one officially infected with COVID-19,

Sara

D^{ear X,}

Good morning and happy Eid. After all, Eid is still Eid, even if it is accompanied by COVID-19, a headache, and a cough.

I wanted to write to you before making my coffee. I will share it with you. I know you love it when I prepare it by hand. I will take all precautionary measures to avoid transmitting the virus to you. Don't worry, it will be perfect for breakfast on Eid, which, although it did so coyly and sadly, eventually came.

I looked at your photos when I woke up, your face embraced by the tranquillity of Eid and the calmness of Ramadan. Your face is where my smile resides. Your smile is my refuge from the disruption of sensation. The smile drawn on your face restores Eid to its formerly wonderful state.

Here is where I will end my message, take my medications, don fresh clothes, and put on lipstick of the colour I know you love. This Eid is missing lots of things, yet it has gained just as much. At the end of the day, it is still Eid.

Happy Eid,

Sara

Good evening,

Despite these being the days of Eid, they pass in such painful monotony. My headache has gradually begun to recede. It still visits from time to time, but with far less severity than before. Today I woke up later than had been my habit in the past few days, and I could smell smoke. At first I thought the building was on fire, but it was just our neighbours grilling their food on the roof. I felt an immediate need to throw up, and I still feel nauseated now. But the good thing is that I had retrieved some of my olfactory senses, or so I thought, since I smelled nothing but the scent of burning. The Ministry of Health ordered me to sequester myself for fourteen days, which is almost over. I believe I am better. I resist the aches that invade my body every couple of hours, and a disruptive cough still rattles my chest, but that's fine.

During my self-sequestration, I've read a lot about how

to get rid of the headache, which is to say I've read a lot to forget that a global pandemic has landed in my body. My attempts failed most of the time. I skimmed wearily through most of what I read and am unable to recall much of anything, although coming across your name was different. Frequently I have passed over your fleeting questions and your brief amazement when I told you about my infection. You scolded me for my previous adventure, which, in your opinion, was the reason behind my sickness.

I kept saying, "I'm strong, don't worry about me," but in fact, I collapsed every night on my bed, exhausted, anxious, and crying. I need you to tell me that this nightmare is about to come to an end. Even if it's a lie, it will be a white one.

JUNE

D^{ear X,}

Eid has passed. This time witnessed a digital momentum of new dimensions. Our chat threads have become jammed with prolonged conversations, and I was not accustomed to such density. I do not mean that literally, for you were threw me with just a few words. Despite that fact, your words have never been like that. You used to comfort me during my solitude, bringing me back to pre-pandemic times with your sweet words. This time you made me feel like I was in a bad dream or perhaps had absconded from a nightmare.

Imagine if everything we went through was just a dream! If I could open my eyes now to find my window open and unblocked, that no curfew had kept us cooped up at home, and that COVID-19 had not chosen me to prove its existence. Imagine if all these distances, the ones I cry over every day, were nothing but words I'm too afraid to say.

I guess imagination isn't as easy as we used to think, is it?

The one immersed in the world of imagination and dreams,

Sara

D^{ear X,}

I'm in a better state than before. Today I decided to start writing a new piece, and I intend to research societal issues. I feel like I've been absent from everything.

You will say that I've mentioned quitting writing before, but you know all too well that I am so engrossed in writing that it is simply inescapable for me. Writing both heals wounds and inflicts wounds, alleviates some pains and aggravates others, but it has a one-way gate: once you step into its realms, there is no exit.

I forgot to tell you that I received a message indicating the end of my sequestration. I can go back to my normal life, which has not been normal since I boarded up my window, but we must be optimistic, right?

In fact, optimism is a relative concept, which I do not think I have embraced recently. I rather doubt I have ever embraced it. I mean, what ray of optimism is discernible in the current circumstances? The whole world is on edge. Madness has possessed everything.

Anyway, an official source has indicated that lockdown will be fully removed soon. Everyone wants the adventure of going out, but I beg you not to. I want to be optimistic, but anxiety has eaten away at me for so long.

Send me a message. Thank God for my recovery. A message from you is all that I need now.

Good evening, dear X,

The curfew has been totally lifted. The pandemic, however, is not over yet: it still roams the streets, looking for bodies to reap. But life was fading away from the city, and something needed to be done to end that. The pandemic counts on those who are not afraid of infection, while the official relies on those who do. Chaos had come to prevail in homes, hearts, and minds alike. The question now is whether hugs will return to gather the people who are scared.

I have contemplated that closed window; I forgot how the light used to penetrate it. I thought of removing the boards, since what I feared had already happened, so what was left to keep me from taking them off? Nevertheless, I'm concerned about what the outside world looks like now. I don't want to look at it, even from behind the bars of my window. I fear that looking at the city would stoke my feelings of sympathy towards it, or towards myself amid your absence.

Do you think anyone else has boarded up their windows like I have?

Good morning X,

Does love really make miracles? Do these miracles make you a prophet? Or is the lover given a thing with prophetic traits?

I know I tend to ask out-of-the-blue questions, but that is no longer surprising, I guess.

Only now do I realize that miracles died out with the absence of prophets. As love is a mere coincidence, a beautiful event surrounded by some lies we willingly choose to believe, and then we feel sad and disappointed when we realize that the whole thing was no more than happenstance and far from being a miracle.

Do you know what I believe?

Love is one form of death. It spreads through your body swiftly, possessing your organs one after another until it makes you feel that there is a heart in every part of you, and little by little these hearts start turning grey. At first there are twinges of pain, and then all of these hearts shatter, dissolving into a recurring death that makes itself felt whenever you breathe, speak, or even smile. So you stop doing those things, exactly as if you were dead. Every question raised in this regard is absurd and has no definitive answer.

The eternal seeker of answers,

Sara

G ood morning,

In this letter, I will include a confession.

I cried a little over you before falling asleep and felt the tears piercing my cheeks. I was filling my mouth with reproachful words so I could spew them out at your face when the malaise of COVID-19 eventually disappears, and when the gloom of your absence from my heart can be pushed away. I could have never imagined that missing you would wake me up one day. Your presence was a matter of fact, and I always took it for granted, so I felt assured. But now it is drowning me in perplexity, even in my sleep.

It is four o'clock in the morning, and I itch to revive our desolate chat, to plant some words of yearning, or perhaps ask a passing question. Would the ambiance of the dawn be an excuse to say, "Isn't the weather wonderful?" Such a question is so false though, because I never cared about the weather. It's just an illogical question. Why would I care about the weather when people are asleep? I would bet that you, however, are still awake. You've been a night-owl for as long as I've known you, sleeping at sunrise, then complaining of headaches and wasted time later. You will not trouble yourself to answer the phone when my name appears on your screen though, or perhaps it won't if the notifications have been disabled.

Is it possible that I'm making serious attempts to revive our chats, and yet no response appears from your side?

Finally, I confess that I am sick of constantly looking for excuses to justify your absence. I'm tired of asking questions. Can questions be viable when the answers have run out?

The very tired,

Sara

JULY

D^{ear X,}

I read a statement in a book today which asserted that the writer tells lies in the search for truth.

What is your opinion about that?

Do you think writing is a figment of mendacity? Doesn't the truth lie inside the books?

If that statement is accurate, it means that bookstores are buzzing with lies, liars, and promoters of lying, not forgetting the buyers of course, who pay money in return for lies. This is scary, as it includes my name in the list of liars for the sake of writing!

I have spent a long time thinking about that statement. Lying is a broad activity, including all that art, literature, and life underline. The world is full of liars.

I think the truth fears the light, in which it might be wrapped, and that makes it relative from one person to another. Anyway, we count on mendacity, exactly like when you say you love me, but in reality, you do not!

G ood evening X,

I had a conversation with a writer this morning. He is one of my colleagues, if I may say. I know you abhor the idea of me talking to a stranger, as if you were afraid he could snatch a smile from my lips, even if it was a transient one. You would rebuke and blame me every time I told you about a similar situation. But I love your jealous rage. Each time you furrow your brow, I sneak a cunning smile.

I don't want to further dwell on this point and make this letter into an explicit flirtation with your rage and jealousy, so I will turn back to that chat with the writer, during which I had a bizarre sensation.

He said that we humans would not be the same as we were before the pandemic because it had created new attributes in us, and that the present is a time of great losses. Here I am, despite my relentless attempts to spread the idea of the lost love in that era, worrying about how accurate his statement was.

I have never thought that we would experience such a pandemic and never imagined that I would count you among the things I fear losing, not after having wagered so much on your steadiness and permanence.

How scared I was to open my eyes and suddenly find out that I have lost you!

The very scared,
Sara

D^{ear X,}

Do you know how the famous writer Al-Jahiz died?

What a strange way to begin, I know, but surely you have got used to such peculiar starts from me.

This question popped into my head when I was about to empty the shelves in my library to start rearranging my books. I bear the responsibility to read, but I fear books will bear the burden of my end. Al-Jahiz died when a stack of his books fell over on top of him. He placed great trust in his beloved books, never suspecting that they would cause his end. That incident proved that what you trust the most and reveal your secrets and true self to might kill you! The death of Al-Jahiz is what we call the irony of fate. Many of us can witness the same thing in our daily lives when we empty our hearts into someone else's; we might as well give them a remote control over our lives when we do that.

I have also seen this happen when I tell you that I fear your absence, but then you disappear, and that makes me think: do you do that on purpose, to prove to yourself that you are free of all constraints? Or to give me a reason to disappear in return?

Anyhow, I am no longer trusting, even of my books.

Sara

D ear X,

Have I told you that I do not like the colour white?

I hate choices that perplex me, and I don't like to choose between two colours as though with a certainty that life is either entirely white or totally black. I very much believe in the greyness of things, and the greyness of people as well. I believe in all colours – except for white.

I think you are blue like the sea you love, but you have no limits and no bottom, which makes you as scary as can be. You might also have some grey tones, some greenness, and perhaps the colour of the night might be reflected in you as well, but you have never been white. And neither have I.

What if the pandemic looted all the colours from the earth and left only whiteness behind to invade the globe? What if all of us became like the victims in the Portuguese author José Saramago's novel "Blindness," unable to see anything but absolute whiteness? What if that whiteness coated the world and doused it in the horrific clamour of light?

I will try to sleep for a bit. These thoughts are causing me a wearisome insomnia, and my attempts to paraphrase the questions put me in an endless labyrinth. From now on I will put the books I finish in a locked box, so their characters will not haunt me like ghosts in the dark. I feel like the doctor from "Blindness" is standing behind me right now, gazing at me despite his blindness, unable to see me, but his wife – the only character who retains her sight – is next to him, eyeing me sharply.

By the way, which colour shades your longing for me?

Dear X,

I am aware that I have stopped writing to you – not for any specific reason, but because I had begun to repeat myself, even though I could not express everything, and I still have more to say. The alphabet at my disposal has finally disappointed me.

I cannot figure out a way to respond to the scarce words that I receive so intermittently from you. I wonder why you do that. Why do you talk to me like a stranger? Yesterday I stopped to think carefully about your brief message, in particular when you asked how I was doing. I preferred to skip this question and leave it unanswered. There is no point in such a question anyway. Why would you care about my health or how I feel after all this absence, and what sort of answer do you think you would receive? Would I tell you that I'm still on your waiting list? Or should I cut it short and say that I'm fine, as this is the typically expected answer? Despite all this confusion, I say with certainty that once I find the answers I'm looking for, everything will be resolved, although this will take our relationship to a horrendous stage.

G ood evening,

I really miss your messages, even those fleeting ones which don't require any response from me.

Where are you?

What a broad question! Very broad indeed, rather as wide as the gap between us.

Let me tell you that there is nothing wrong with sending empty messages, for they are still messages.

I tried earnestly not to leave our chat thirsty for messages, but it gets even thirstier every time a message is sent and remains on your unanswered waiting list. I am confused, unable to decide what I should do. Shall I continue sending messages and making excuses? Or should I stop until you become aware of my empty space?

These questions overwhelm me, accumulating to form an inner burning urge to scream. My persistent hopes for you have drained my soul. Has the time come to break the threads that bind us together? I am terribly confused, very sad, and extremely tired – tired of you, of me, of my throat that started to make me feel like I was suffocating, of the letters that are piling up in every corner of my home, and of that world that is still stalking me, just beyond my boarded-up window.

If only you could appear at this moment as a comet in my bleak sky!

The very tired,

Sara

AUGUST

Dear X,

I have received your message yesterday; it was one of those messages that pop up to aggravate my desire to cry! This message arrived after nearly a month of inexcusable and unjustified estrangement.

When my phone lit up to announce the appearance of your name, many sensations engulfed me, so many it would be difficult to count after so much waiting. You came up with a five-line summary of an absence that I have never experienced before. I was stuck between crying and pathetic happiness!

I wonder: what would you have written if your message was to be delivered by a postman? Would you send a sheet of paper with only five lines? Would I curse the postman who delivered it late, or curse you, who could not bear the burden of writing earlier?

I remain perplexed when it comes to expressing my longing for you, which suffocates me every time I wait for you and you don't show up, or you appear only partially, so I start searching relentlessly for your other half, even though I showed up with my whole being – and then some!

The very confused,

Sara

Good morning,

You vanished as if you had never existed, and all it took was to send you a sharply and harshly worded admonishment, to plant a cactus in our abandoned chat, and to ask you where I was in you!

You were slowly stripping me off of you, thinking that I wouldn't notice until I found myself sloughed off. My vigilance startled you, so you favoured long silence.

You have left me facing a predicament of the questions that I was full of, those I despaired of resolving. I seriously tried to shut the door, which I had left ajar, hoping you would return through it. But it was heavy, so heavy that I could not push it. Nor could I sleep afterwards, as the night felt terribly long.

I have not received a single word from you for another whole month. I used to scroll through our chat every morning, thinking of the wonderful mornings that we shared. And now all I think about is my inability to wipe them out of my head.

I feel like my tears have gone on forever, yet my words are still insufficient to reach the peak of my soul, unable to reach the destination I have assigned them. I try hard. I send you prolonged messages, but you do not read them. I try again with a shorter one, yet you leave it, too, unread.

Don't the mornings pass heavily on you, as they pass on me? Or might they not pass at all?

SEPTEMBER

Dear X,

I had to figure out that your few messages were a breakup omen, that your courage had let you down, so you couldn't pass this message to me directly, so you preferred to deliver the separation message through a long silence. However, this is nothing but fear, your fear of my detachment, but somehow your fear of my closeness as well.

Tell me, for God's sake, what steps are left that I have not taken towards you yet? Do you fear my grief when you favoured my abandonment? Or do you fear the sadness that might visit you after my departure?

Don't worry. I don't intend to cause problems. I will preserve my silence. I might cry over you for a long time, but you will not know that. Perhaps I will write a novel about you and kill you in it, but I don't think you'll ever read any more of my messages or anything that has my name on it, even though you know that our names are inseparable. You know that my ghost will haunt you every step of the way. It will accompany you in the alleys. You will remember that we laughed there and walked here, had dinner at your favourite restaurant, made a vow to stay together, and that we are together even if we were not!

I know that you will damn me deep inside, and I will do that too. I know very well that no woman will ever love you as much as I did or tolerate you as much as I did.

OCTOBER

DEAR X

G ood morning, or good evening maybe ... whatever,

Dear X, my love, my friend, my journey companion, and all my beautiful and sorrowful things. This is my last letter to you. The scourge which befell the world like raining acid has not ended yet, but here, at this point, I will stop writing paper letters. I will collect them all in a locked box with a red seal bearing my name, so you can recognize me after a period of absence, the eventual duration of which I have no clue. Hopefully, you will realize one day that I really was there with you. In fact, it is with sorrow that I will stop writing to you. I know you will not read my paper letters, but in case you refresh our deserted chat with a question, I will tell you that I am just tired and need a worrier's rest. It will be a long rest indeed, during which I hope not to write about you. I do not promise to do that, though, since I am, as you well know, so vulnerable and fragile before your smile. However, I will try my best to stop.

Oh, X, Oh, my love! For that last time, I want to shout out loud and call you "my love." You were the one who inhabited every organ of my body, you stayed so long that you took root deep inside me like a stubborn tree against the erosion of time. A month after the outbreak of the pandemic and the virus's invasion of so many hearts and minds before actual bodies, I realized that my own roots had not been sufficiently ingrained in your soil. The winds of abandonment have plucked them out, and this tears my heart apart, but I am helpless, and my hands are tied, aren't they?

Oh, X! My darling, do you know how I feel at this moment? I feel light, like a balloon that was relieved of all its ballast so it flew and rambled in the sky directionless, floating among the clouds that hold no rain ... this lightness with all its hideous meaning.

I am terribly sad for what has happened to our souls, for all those days when you assured me that you were staying by my side no matter what, and that my place would remain as it was, whatever shapes our days took. Does anyone have the right to promise permanence when they are ignorant of what the future will bring? Do you remember those words, dear X? Do you recall all that, my love, on whose sincerity I always wagered? Please rely on me, for I will always be with

DEAR X

you, my love.

I crave to repeat this word, "love," which my shyness once restrained me from saying in your presence. This word I have never used this way for a being other than you. I will write it until I run out of ink, as the past time between us could not help me say it. I want to hear its echo in my chest, to include it in my special vocabulary, and I really want you to know that I mean it – with all the meaning this word can hold.

My love, X, you are running, and I am tenderly running after you. You would not deign to pause for my sake. I feel that I have run for ages, without rest, towards a destiny, and always you remained far from my reach, even when I thought I was almost there. I will stop on the side of the road. I will not wait, yet I will stay there to pray for you, for a coincidence that might make our paths cross again.

This is me, with all the weariness I carry.

202?

It was shortly after dawn and the wooden boards leaned against the wall as though they were tired from having stood for too long. The window was wide open, which allowed the sun to fully occupy the room and flood it with light. There was a cup of tea on the table next to a Portuguese novel and some sheets of paper with yellowish edges. The sounds of a local accent resonated with the place, courtesy of a television series. Sara was reclined on the couch and gazing silently at the television, but she paid little attention to the actors as they argued over nickels and dimes and a love relationship they thought was real.

After the episode ended, she got up to make a cup of coffee, as her tea had cooled before she took a single sip. She tightened her lips around the edge of the cup and closed her eyes. She felt like she was flying in a cloudless sky, but she descended quickly to the ground when she heard a knock on the door, and slowly stepped towards it. She got very close to the door, then leaned back when the knocking stopped. She wondered if she was delusional, but then the knocking resumed, so she opened the door to look.

"Sara!"

She could not say anything and just stood there, stunned. Her throat completely dried out, and the pupils of her eyes widened as though she were looking at an old ghost.

"What are you doing here?" she finally asked in a halting voice

"You stopped answering my messages. Why? And why is your phone line cut? I tried reaching out many times, but you've changed your address. It took me months to finally find you."

"How did you find me?"

"I never stopped searching for you."

"Why?"

"Will you leave me hanging at the door?"

"Yes."

His next question stopped at his throat, so she continued in a low voice, "Do you know how much time has passed?"

"You ran away from me whenever I tried to reach out!"

"Yes ... I know."

"Why?"

"Because many things have changed."

"That was enough for me not to return, but I did."

"But you returned." She repeated his words slowly as she

retrieved an age of absence from her memory.

She left him at the door and headed to a bookshelf which stood along the wall behind some chairs. She took down a box, wiped some dust off its surface with her fingers, walked back to the door, and handed it to him.

"Here you go."

"What is this?"

"Your messages to me. I used to print them out and reply with paper letters."

"But I've never received anything from you!"

"I know. I've never sent any."

"Sara!"

"Here they are, right in your hands now. Read them and come back to me. I'll be waiting for you."

She closed the door.

The End